A NOTE TO PAREN

Reading Aloud with Your Child

Research shows that reading books aloud is the single most valuable support parents can provide in helping children learn to read.

- Be a ham! The more enthusiasm you display, the more your child will enjoy the book.
- Run your finger underneath the words as you read to signal that the print carries the story.
- Leave time for examining the illustrations more closely; encourage your child to find things in the pictures.
- Invite your youngster to join in whenever there's a repeated phrase in the text.
- Link up events in the book with similar events in your child's life.
- If your child asks a question, stop and answer it. The book can be a means to learning more about your child's thoughts.

Listening to Your Child Read Aloud

The support of your attention and praise is absolutely crucial to your child's continuing efforts to learn to read.

- If your child is learning to read and asks for a word, give it immediately so that the meaning of the story is not interrupted. DO NOT ask your child to sound out the word.
- On the other hand, if your child initiates the act of sounding out, don't intervene.
- If your child is reading along and makes what is called a miscue, listen for the sense of the miscue. If the word "road" is substituted for the word "street," for instance, no meaning is lost. Don't stop the reading for a correction.
- If the miscue makes no sense (for example, "horse" for "house"), ask your child to reread the sentence because you're not sure you understand what's just been read.
- Above all else, enjoy your child's growing command of print and make sure you give lots of praise. *You are your child's first teacher — and the most important one. Praise from you is critical for further risk-taking and learning.*

— Priscilla Lynch
Ph.D., New York University
Educational Consultant

Go Philipstown Seahawks!
—J.M.

Go Warner Wildcats!
—T.K.

Text copyright © 1997 by Jean Marzollo.
Illustrations copyright © 1997 by True Kelley.
All rights reserved. Published by Scholastic Inc.
HELLO READER! and CARTWHEEL BOOKS and associated logos
are trademarks and/or registered trademarks of Scholastic Inc.

Library of Congress Cataloging-in-Publication Data

Marzollo, Jean.
    Football friends / by Jean Marzollo; illustrated by True Kelley.
        p.   cm.— (Hello reader! Level 3)
    Summary: When he plays football at school, Freddy has trouble avoiding fights, until he uses his anger to play better.
    ISBN 0-590-38395-7
    [1. Football—Fiction. 2. Anger—Fiction.]
I. Kelley, True, ill. II. Title. III. Series.
PZ7.M3688Fo   1997
[E]—dc21
                                                        97-9096
                                                        CIP
                                                        AC

12 11 10 9 8 7 6 5 4 3 2

Printed in the U.S.A.   24
First printing, October 1997

Football
Friends

by Jean, Dan, and Dave Marzollo

Illustrated by True Kelley

Hello Reader! — Level 3

SCHOLASTIC INC.
New York Toronto London Auckland Sydney

"Let's play touch football. I'll be a captain," said Freddy.

"Me, too," said Mark. "I pick Carlos."

"Why did you go first?" asked Freddy.

"Because I did," said Mark.

Freddy was mad. He wanted Carlos because Carlos had the best throwing arm.

"I pick Tommy," said Freddy.

"Sara," said Mark.

"No fair!" said Freddy. He wanted Sara on his team.

"Is too," said Mark.

"Is not," said Freddy. "I quit."

"You're a baby," said Mark.

Freddy jumped on Mark and threw him to the ground. Mark fought back. Freddy got dirt in his mouth and a bump on his head.

Suddenly a whistle blew. An aide came over. "Freddy and Mark, to the office," she said.

Freddy and Mark were mad as tigers.

"Fighting again?" asked Mrs. Smith. She was the principal.

"Freddy knocked me over," said Mark.

"Mark called me a baby," said Freddy.

Mrs. Smith looked at them. "What's the difference between a big boy and a baby?" she asked.

Freddy and Mark didn't know what to say.

"This is a baby," said Mrs. Smith. She waved her arms and made baby noises.

Mark and Freddy began to laugh.

Mrs. Smith laughed, too. "I'm glad we got that straight. Now tell me. What were you two really fighting about?"

"We were going to play football," said Freddy. "Mark and I were captains. But it wasn't fair. He had the better team. So I quit. That's when he called me a baby."

"And that's when you lost your temper," said Mrs. Smith. She looked worried. "Is football too rough for you to play?"

"No!" said both boys. "We use a foam ball, and we just play touch. No one tackles. No one gets hurt."

Mrs. Smith smiled. "I'm glad that you two agree on something. And usually you are friends, right?"

"Right," said Freddy and Mark.

"Then why do you always fight when you play this game?" she asked.

Freddy pointed to Mark. "He always gets the better team."

"*He* always loses his temper," said Mark.

"That's because the teams are uneven," said Freddy.

"I have an idea," said Mrs. Smith. "I'm going to give you football homework. I want you to work on it together. Your job is to make two even teams."

That night Freddy and Mark talked on the phone. Their homework was hard, but they did it.

The next day they gave their lists to Mrs. Smith.

COWBOYS	RAIDERS
Freddy	Mark
Sara	Carlos
Tommy	Matteo
Zak	Kim
Dontay	Casey

Recess came. Kids met on the playground to play touch football. Mrs. Smith came, too. She showed the kids the chart.

"Are these teams fair?" she asked.

"Yes," said the kids.

"Fine," said Mrs. Smith. "Then you may play touch football. But you must use these teams. And if there is any more fighting, there will be no more football. Do you understand?"

Everyone said yes.

The teams got set. Mark and Freddy were opposite each other. The game began.

Freddy hiked the ball to Tommy. Tommy flipped it to Sara. The ball bounced off her hands. It flew into the air.

Freddy caught it before it hit the ground.

He ran all the way to the pavement and scored!

The Cowboys were ahead 7–0. Each touchdown was worth seven points. There were no extra points in their playground game.

The Raiders now had the ball. Mark hiked the ball to Carlos. Carlos ran to the left. He saw Mark on the other side of the field. Carlos threw a pass to Mark.

Mark caught it and ran toward the end zone.

Freddy ran as fast as he could after him. He wished he could run faster. He didn't want Mark to score.

Freddy finally caught up with Mark. Freddy reached out to touch him. There! He touched him!

But Mark kept running. He crossed the goal line.

"Touchdown!" Mark shouted.

"No way!" cried Freddy. "I touched you!"

"You did not!" yelled Mark. "I didn't feel a thing!"

Freddy ran at Mark and started to push him.

"Cut it out, Freddy!" said Sara. "Mrs. Smith is watching. Don't you remember what she said? If there's fighting, no more football."

Freddy let up. But he was still mad.

The score was now 7–7, and recess was almost over.

Freddy wanted to win!

The Cowboys and the Raiders lined up.
Freddy and Mark were face-to-face.
"You're going to lose," said Mark,
"because you're a baby. I can say whatever I
want because now you can't fight me."

Freddy gave Mark a shove.

"Time out!" said Tommy. "Huddle up, team!"

The Cowboys formed a circle.

"Freddy, keep your cool!" hissed Sara.

"He called me a baby," said Freddy. "What am I supposed to do? Say thank you?"

Sara was disgusted. "He's just trying to get you mad so you won't play well."

"Don't pay any attention to Mark," said Tommy. "Use your anger to run faster. Okay?"

The teams lined up.

"Baby," said Mark. "Ga-ga. Goo-goo!"

This really made Freddy mad. But instead of hitting Mark, he thought about Sara's words: *He's just trying to get you mad so you won't play well.* Her words made sense.

Then he remembered what Tommy had said. *Use your anger to run faster.*

"Ga-ga. Goo-goo!" said Mark again.

Freddy pretended he didn't hear. But inside his rage burned. Freddy pretended it was like rocket fuel! He hiked the ball back to Tommy and ran toward the goal. He turned his head to look back.

Tommy aimed and fired. The ball was coming right to Freddy!

Freddy reached up for it.

Freddy caught the ball and brought it down to his chest. Then he ran as fast as he could. He heard footsteps behind him. But Freddy was too fast for anyone to catch. He blasted into the end zone.

"Ga-ga. Goo-goo!" Freddy shouted as he crossed the line.

"Ga-ga. Goo-goo!" sang Sara and Tommy. The Cowboys waved their arms and toddled like babies.

It was the first football game they had won in a long time. It was also the first game without a big fight.

Later, Mrs. Smith stopped Freddy in the
hall. "I want to talk with you," she said.
"I wasn't fighting!" said Freddy.

Mrs. Smith smiled. "I don't only talk to kids when they've done something wrong. Sometimes I talk to them when they have done something right. I heard Mark tease you, and I saw what you did. You almost lost your cool. But then you controlled your temper."

Freddy blushed. "My team helped me," he said.

"That's the way to handle teasers," she said. "If you ignore them, they'll give up teasing you. That's one way to stay out of fights."

Freddy smiled.

"I don't think I'll mind if Mark teases me again," he said. "Thanks to him, I scored a touchdown."